VIKING
Published by the Penguin Group
Penguin Putnam Books for Young Readers, 345 Hudson Street,
New York, New York 10014, U.S.A.
Penguin Books Ltd, 80 Strand, London WC2R 0RL, England
Penguin Books Australia Ltd, Ringwood, Victoria, Australia
Penguin Books Canada Ltd, 10 Alcorn Avenue, Toronto, Ontario, Canada M4V 3B2
Penguin Books (N.Z.) Ltd, 182-190 Wairau Road, Auckland 10, New Zealand

Penguin Books Ltd, Registered Offices: Harmondsworth, Middlesex, England

Published in 2002 by Viking,
a division of Penguin Putnam Books for Young Readers.

1 3 5 7 9 10 8 6 4 2

LIBRARY OF CONGRESS CATALOGING-IN-PUBLICATION DATA
Bartlett, Susan.
The Seal Island seven / by Susan Bartlett ; illustrated by Tricia Tusa.
p.   cm.
Summary: When Pru and her friends find out that someone on the island is
destroying fairy houses, they set out to find the culprit.
ISBN 0-670-03533-5 (hardcover)
[1. One-room schools—Fiction. 2. Schools—Fiction. 3. Islands—Fiction.
4. Maine—Fiction.] I. Tusa, Tricia, ill. II. Title.
PZ7.W3896 Sf 2002   [Fic]—dc21   2001006307

Printed in U.S.A.
Set in Baskerville, Minya

For Elise, Nick, and Alex
—S. B.

THE SEAL
ISLAND SEVEN

by Susan Bartlett ✪ illustrated by Tricia Tusa

VIKING

CONTENTS

CHAPTER ONE

SURPRISE PACKAGES

Pru Stanley was too excited to sit still. She stood up on her chair. "I'm so glad we're back!" She waved at her teacher.

"I'm excited, too." Miss Sparling walked between the rows, handing out lumpy silver-paper packages the size of soup cans. "But get down, Pru, before you fall." A Newfoundland dog followed her. His huge tail thwacked back and forth against the desks.

"Gander's happy school has started." Pru slid into her seat. "Can he come every day?" The dog had been her idea. She had helped raise money to buy him for her teacher last spring.

"If he learns 'sit' and 'stay.'" Miss Sparling gave Pru a package. "And 'no drooling.'"

"Especially the last." Nicholas, Pru's best friend, patted Gander on the head. "He needs a bib."

Gander nuzzled Nicholas's leg and sat down beside his chair.

"We'll open our surprises in a minute," said Miss Sparling, stepping around the dog. "They're in honor of our new students." She smiled at Clara and Sophie Hall.

Three days ago Captain Hill's boat had made a special trip from the mainland, bringing the Hall family, their furniture, Sophie's pet turtle, and Clara's cat to Seal Island.

"I was at the ferry when it unloaded their stuff," Harry Smith said. He was in the sixth grade and liked to know everything that happened on the island.

"I saw you at the dock." Clara stood up and

made a bow. "Hi! I'm Clara. I'm in fourth grade."

"You're the first person ever in my grade." Pru felt like clapping.

"And, as everyone knows, this is Sophie," said Miss Sparling.

"I'm the only first grader," Sophie said. "Hooray for me!"

"I wouldn't brag about it." Clara leaned over and poked her sister.

"We were in the first grade last year," Doug Miller said. "Me and him." He pointed to Max Day, whose pet ferret slept in a cage by his feet.

"The Seal Island seven," Nicholas announced from the back row. "A gargantuan group."

"He likes big words," Pru told Clara.

"I'm impressed," said Clara. She waved her package. "May we open our presents now?" At Miss Sparling's nod, she tore off the silver wrapping. Inside was a wooden lighthouse painted white and blue with yellow windowpanes.

"It's the Seal Island lighthouse," said Max. "I can tell."

"I made them for you this summer," Miss Sparling explained.

"Cool!" said Doug. He liked to collect feathers and fish bones. "Maybe I'll start collecting lighthouses."

Miss Sparling held up a lighthouse of her own. "Let's keep these on our desks to remind us how lucky we are to have a new family on the island. They can be our good luck talismans."

"I believe in good luck charms," said Pru, happy that Miss Sparling had made her a present. "Especially four-leaf clovers."

"I believe in magic," Doug told everyone. "One time I saw a rabbit come right out of a hat."

"I can explain that." Nicholas raised his hand.

"Maybe a little later," Miss Sparling said quickly.

"Thank you for the present," Pru said, convinced her teacher was the nicest in Maine.

"Thank you, Miss Sparling," repeated the rest of the class.

"You're welcome." Miss Sparling set down her lighthouse. "Now, each day we begin with a story." She picked up a book with a pink and green cover. "Because books are—" she began in a loud voice. Then she stopped and waited.

"—the golden key that opens the enchanted door." Everyone except Sophie and Clara knew the answer by heart.

"I know that book," Doug exclaimed as Miss Sparling held up *Burt Dow, Deepwater Man.* "It's about Maine."

Everyone listened quietly while Miss Sparling read.

"I liked that," said Sophie when the story ended.

"Me, too," said Pru.

"That's good, because with five different grades this year—" Miss Sparling stopped to take a breath.

"—we have to cooperate," Nicholas finished for her.

"I can help," said Harry. "I'm the oldest and wisest."

"Then you get to read with Max and Doug." Miss Sparling gave the second graders their books. "Everyone else, silent reading for thirty minutes while I work with Sophie."

After reading, Pru, Nicholas, Clara, and Harry moved with their math worksheets to a table in the corner.

"This sure is different from my school in Cranberry Cove," Clara said.

"My fourth grade in New York had twenty-five kids," Nicholas told them. "I couldn't believe it when I moved here last year."

"He didn't like it at first," explained Pru.

Nicholas finished one row of problems and started another. "My parents thought it would be great to live on an island." He groaned. "They dragged me here."

"Bummer!" Clara said. "At least I'd been here before with my dad. I wanted to move here." She looked around the room. "Do you have music? There's no piano."

"Miss Sparling plays the guitar. And we sing." Pru wanted Clara to like the school. "Max's mom brings her autoharp."

"How about gym?" Clara lowered her voice

when she saw Miss Sparling put a finger to her lips.

"We have a baseball field," said Harry. "And track meets." He erased an answer, tearing a hole in his paper.

"I still remember what you told us in your letter," Pru said to Clara. "The one I found on the beach in the bottle. 'I wish I lived on an island,' you wrote."

"It was fate," said Nicholas. "Look what happened. Here you are."

"Well, it was really because my dad needed a fishing job."

"I'm glad you came." Nicholas made a thumbs-up sign. "Variety is the spice of life."

What's *that* supposed to mean? Pru asked herself. It sounded strange. Was Nicholas looking for a new friend? Was he bored with her? Maybe he thought Clara was "spicier" because she was new.

"Finished?" asked Miss Sparling.

Pru collected the math papers and sat down on the rug with everyone else to share stories of the summer. She had such a good time describing her camping trip to Mount Katahdin that her uneasy feeling slipped away. Of course she and Nicholas would always be best friends, and to have Clara come to the island was extra special. Like chocolate sprinkles and marshmallow sauce on ice cream, two friends would be a double treat.

CHAPTER TWO

A SPECIAL PLACE

Pru stepped onto her front porch with two balloons and a pocketful of fudge. It was Saturday morning and she was going to Clara's house for the first time. "Bye," she yelled to her parents. Then in one arching jump she and her dog Schooner sailed over the steps and landed on the soggy grass. All morning an early fall storm had spattered the island with rain.

"Clara's my new friend," Pru told Schooner as they splashed in the puddles. "She's nice, but she doesn't have a dog for you. Only a cat."

They stopped before a big, white house in a yard littered with packing boxes. From the roof of the second story rose a round tower topped with a weathervane.

"I'll be back." Pru patted Schooner's head and secured his leash to the ring of an anchor that lay beside the path. He shook himself and sat down.

She knocked on the front door, which stood partway open. "Hi, Pru. Come on in." Mrs. Hall smiled. "Clara's upstairs in the cupola."

Pru hung her wet raincoat on a peg and climbed to the second story. From the hall a ladder led to an opening in the ceiling.

"Come on up!" Clara's face appeared in the hole, her straight red hair falling over her face.

Pru let go of her balloons and Clara reached out to grab them. "These are for you," Pru said.

"Thanks!" Clara held out her other hand to help Pru over the last rung. "Isn't this place great?"

"Wow!" Pru stared at the windows all around her. "We're so high. I've never been in a cupola before. I feel like I might tip over." She walked a few steps to the edge of the room. "Hey! I can see my house." Her dad was carrying a lobster trap across the yard to his storage shed. From another window, she could see Gull Rock at the harbor entrance and the island ferry as it cut through the waves toward the dock, spilling foam on both sides of its bow.

Clara looped the balloon strings around a nail in the wall. "There's Clam." She pointed to her cat in the dirt road. "He loves it here, because there aren't any cars. Boy, is that weird!"

Pru didn't think that having no cars was weird at all. Three old pickups carried the fishing gear to and from the wharf and the supplies from the ferry to the store. She walked or rode her pony, Velvet, wherever she wanted to go.

"And no electricity is even weirder," Clara went on. "I'm getting used to it, though, and gas lights are kind of fun." She reached out her arms as if to embrace the space. "Mom and

Dad said I could have this room."

"Fantastic! Will they let you sleep up here?"

Clara shook her head. "There's not enough room for a bed. I have to sleep downstairs with Sophie, the pest. We're lucky she's out playing or she'd be bugging us."

Pru thought it would be nice to have a sister. Maybe she and Clara could be like sisters. She imagined how much fun they could have. "I bet the lighthouse shines in at night. Sleeping up here would be awesome."

"Maybe you could stay over sometime," Clara said. "We could put sleeping bags on the floor."

"If you want, I'll bring my Parcheesi board. Dad made it for me. We can play together." Pru reached in her pocket. "Want some fudge? I made it this morning."

Clara popped a piece in her mouth. "Peanut butter! My favorite."

"Mine, too." Now Pru knew they would get along perfectly.

Outside, as they watched, the trees at the edge of Deep Woods swayed in the wind and rain. "Is that where we built fairy houses when I came in May to visit?" Clara asked.

Pru nodded. Ever since she was four, she had built fairy houses out of twigs, put pennies inside, and made wishes.

"Did your wishes ever come true?" Clara wanted to know.

"I wished you'd move here. And you did. That was my best wish."

Clara stepped back from the window and smiled at Pru. "Maybe this time I'll build something really special. A fairy garden. Or a palace for the queen."

Pru thought a palace would be wonderful. "No one's ever done *that*."

"I like to build things. I'm going to be an architect when I grow up. Last year I built a Lego skyscraper and won first prize in a contest."

"Look!" said Pru. "Out there!"

At the edge of the trees, a boy in a yellow slicker stopped and beckoned to someone behind him to hurry up. "Isn't that Nicholas?" Clara asked. "He is so cute."

Cute? thought Pru. Nicholas was . . . well, Nicholas was her best friend. She never thought about him being cute. "Yup, that's him," she said. "That's Picasso, his poodle. And Doug and Max. I wonder why they're running."

"And there's Sophie! What's she doing with them?"

"Maybe they're going to meet the boat. Want to walk down? I have to help unload hay bales for Velvet."

"Sure." Clara started down the ladder. "Doesn't school get boring?" she asked unexpectedly. "Just one room?"

"It's two rooms," Pru corrected her. "One has supplies. And it's *not* boring."

"At my last school we had sixteen kids in just third and fourth grade."

So? Pru liked her school just the way it was. Well, maybe one or two more kids would be fun, but lots? No way. She hoped Clara wouldn't be homesick for her old school. Before she could say anything more, Schooner barked, and someone pounded on the front door and yelled her name.

CHAPTER THREE

TROUBLE IN THE WOODS

"Pru!" Nicholas's voice came through the door.

Just as Pru and Clara reached the bottom step, Nicholas and Sophie burst into the front hall. Max and Doug were close behind.

"What's the matter?" Pru asked.

Nicholas caught his breath. "We were in the woods. We ran all the way back. Guess what?"

"A monster!" shrieked Sophie.

"A what?" asked Clara.

"Not a monster." Nicholas glared at Sophie. "But something scary."

"Scary how?" Clara wanted to know.

"We were going to show Sophie how to make fairy houses," Doug said.

Sophie held up a penny. "I was all ready."

"In the rain?" asked Clara.

"We got to this flat place where we always go—" Doug stopped.

"And a whole bunch of the houses were smashed," Max said. "Like this." He swung one foot in a fast kick.

"Sticks and moss were all over," Doug added, waving his arms.

"With bottlecaps and stones and stuff." Nicholas held up a tangle of pink yarn.

"That's awful." Pru couldn't imagine who would knock down a fairy house. If anything bad happened to a house, the fairy wouldn't grant your wish. "Maybe it was a deer."

Max shook his head. "We didn't see any tracks."

"Or it could have been a dog." Pru was sure there must be an explanation. Everyone had probably been too excited to see any clues.

"Hey!" Max's eyes grew wider. "I saw a new dog get off the ferry yesterday."

Doug made a circle with his thumb and finger. "Bull's-eye! That guy with all the cameras."

"My mom told me he's photographing the island for a magazine," said Nicholas. "He took her picture because she's president of Save the Whales."

"What if his dog did it?" Pru felt her face grow hot, like it did when she got mad. No one had a right to knock over fairy houses. It took a long time to build a good one. "I'm making a sign: LEASH YOUR DOG OR ELSE!" She turned to Clara. "It's the rule here, especially when you go into the woods."

"Can we get him arrested?" asked Max.

"We need evidence first." Doug liked to pretend he was a detective.

"We'll hide in the woods and collect evidence," Pru said.

"Maybe we should talk to the photographer first," Nicholas suggested.

"Criminals never admit they're guilty." Doug was certain.

"I'm not doing it." Sophie's voice rose. "Ask Clara. She's not scared of anything."

"I am, too," Clara disagreed. "I'm scared of monster movies and jellyfish. Why don't we spy on him from the cupola?"

"Superexcellent idea!" said Nicholas.

"Follow me!" Clara led the way to the stairs and then to the top of the ladder. One by one, everybody stepped into the cupola's round space.

"Extraordinary!" Nicholas exclaimed when he saw the room.

Doug pressed his nose to the glass. "Look, everyone! There's my house."

"We've seen your house a million times," said Nicholas. "We're looking for clues." He took the binoculars that Clara handed him and focused on the harbor road.

"Could we have a secret club here?" asked Max. "With passwords?"

"It's Clara's special place," Pru protested, not wanting to share it with everyone so soon.

"My parents don't want anyone to fall through the hole," Clara said. "I have to be careful."

"Careful about whom to invite, you mean," Nicholas teased. "Discriminating."

Clara smiled at him. "It's okay if *you* come."

Oh? thought Pru. She grabbed the binoculars from Nicholas. "Hey! There he is!" A man with a dog turned off the road toward Lighthouse Hill. The sun had come out and glinted on the buckles of his camera bags.

"That dog's a Doberman," said Nicholas.

"I'm not going after it," Max said. "Dobermans are scary."

"I'm not either." Sophie started down the ladder. "I'm getting a snack."

"Me, too. Detectives need brain food." Doug stepped in line behind Sophie. "Does your mom have granola bars?" he asked.

"Wimps!" Clara said. "I'm going to follow him."

"I'm with you." Nicholas turned away from the window.

"I'll go first." Pru wasn't going to let Clara take over. After all, she knew the island better than any of them.

CHAPTER FOUR

WHOSE FOOTPRINT?

"Hurry!" Pru ordered, wanting to show she was in charge. She, Nicholas, and Clara sprinted out of the house and up the hill. Sticks snapped and stones tumbled under their feet.

"He'll be able to hear us a mile away," said Nicholas.

"We can't slow down." Pru looked around when they reached the top of the hill. "I don't see anybody. Maybe he took another path."

"This is crazy," said Clara. "He wasn't that far ahead."

Soon they came to the place where the fairy houses lay scattered. Silvery glitter, yarn, and loose seashells littered the ground.

"Unfathomable," said Nicholas.

"He can't figure it out," Clara explained.

"I know what he means." Pru didn't need Clara to explain Nicholas to her. She kicked a tumble of sticks. "Here's where I made the house when you came to visit." She thought back to how excited she had been when she first met Clara and showed her the island.

"I remember. That was fun." Clara moved suddenly to the edge of the mossy circle, bent over, and studied the ground. "Definitely a grown-up," she said.

"What is?" Pru asked.

Clara showed them a footprint. "It's big and

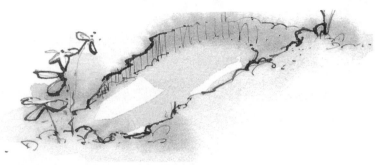

you can see tread marks. Like a hiking boot."

Something rustled the leaves nearby, making them jump.

Two deer walked onto the trail. They stopped a few feet away from Pru.

"They aren't afraid." Clara sounded amazed.

"They're used to me." Pru was proud that the deer trusted her. She loved their gentle eyes and black noses. "The island's so small, we keep meeting."

"Just don't call them Donder and Blitzen," Nicholas said as the deer stepped aside to nibble a spruce branch.

Clara giggled. "I'd never do anything that unoriginal. You're so funny." She looked admiringly at Nicholas.

"It's nothing," Nicholas said.

Really, thought Pru. Then how come he's blushing?

Clara took a folded sheet of paper out of her pocket. "I'll draw the footprint. It's our first stomper clue."

"What for?" asked Pru. "We can't ask the photographer to lift up his shoe so we can compare it."

"Of course not. We'll follow him and look for a footprint that matches the drawing," Clara explained.

"Superexcellent idea!" Nicholas approved.

"What about paw prints?" Pru felt that it was more important to identify the dog. "I don't see any of those."

"First we need to match the footprint." Clara was certain.

"But it had to be a dog," Pru argued. "No person would do something like that."

"We don't know for sure," said Nicholas. "I agree with Clara. Let's keep after him."

"We should look for both," Pru insisted. Clara hadn't even been here a week. She was acting like she knew everything.

They walked on, but there was no further sign of the photographer on the trail. By the time they turned to hike back, the rain had begun again. The footprints on the path were now tiny, muddy pools. Pru was secretly glad. She would find the next clue herself.

Back at Clara's house, Pru said good-bye and headed home with Schooner. On the way she decided to stop at school to get her lucky lighthouse. Even on Saturday, the door was always open. She let herself in, took the lighthouse from her desk, and stuck it in her raincoat pocket. Maybe it would help lead her to the right paw print.

Then she hurried home, hungry for the fish chowder she knew Mom had made for lunch. As soon as she had eaten, she saddled Velvet. I'll look for clues, she thought, and started toward town.

At the intersection of Main Street and the dock road, she looked downhill to the harbor and the afternoon boat, ready for its return trip to Rockland. She liked to watch the ferry come and go. The store truck had delivered its empty bottles and cans for recycling ashore and was turning around. Nearly all the passengers had left the dock and disappeared on board.

Except for one man. She stared. There, with his camera bags and his dog, was the photographer.

Now or never, Pru thought, and kicked Velvet

forward. As soon as they clattered onto the wooden planks of the dock, she dismounted quickly, dropped Velvet's reins around a piling, and ran toward the boat. The man crossed the gangplank. His boots looked big, like the footprint, but she couldn't see enough of them to be sure. Maybe she could solve the mystery right now on her own. She felt the lighthouse in her pocket. All she had to do was ask. Maybe he'd say yes, my dog did it, and I'm really sorry.

The first mate pulled up the gangplank. The boat was ready to leave.

"Did your dog stomp the fairy houses?" Pru yelled.

At just that moment the ferry whistle shrilled. The man opened his mouth to answer, but Pru couldn't hear a thing. The dog barked, the engine roared, and the boat turned into the splashing waves.

CHAPTER FIVE

THE FAIRY PALACE

"Just let someone stomp on this!" Clara threatened several days later. "I'll call the Coast Guard." She had built a fairy palace, three stories high, decorated with tinsel, crimson ribbon, and artificial flowers. She turned to Nicholas. "What do you think?"

Nicholas sat off to one side watching. "It's huge all right. Any bigger and it would fall over."

For the past hour, Pru, Clara, Nicholas, Max, and Doug had been in the woods after school cleaning up the damaged houses and building new ones.

"Is that all you can say?" Clara asked. "It's stupendous."

Pru had to admit it was beautiful. Her own house looked just about big enough for a fairy baby. But she liked to think that fairies preferred little houses, since they were so teeny themselves.

"Your LEASH YOUR DOG sign is cool, Pru." Max picked up a plastic lobster and a handful of bottle caps.

"My dad helped me hammer it in," Pru said. "I've seen lots of paw prints since we started to look. I've seen big footprints, too, but I can't tell whose dogs or whose boots."

"Did you see the fairy house back where the trail divides?" Clara asked. "It didn't get knocked over. It has three stories and a roof garden."

"Pretentious." Nicholas stood up, paced around, and sat down again. "This isn't New York City."

Clara disagreed. "I think it's neat."

"At least we haven't found any more smashed houses since the photographer left." Pru had told them about the meeting on the dock.

"Does that prove the Doberman is the guilty party?" Doug stuffed a soda can into his litter bag.

"Yes! The dog left and the stomping stopped," said Max. "Good detective work."

"I don't know." Clara glanced around them. "Could one dog have done all this?"

Doug nodded. "Yup, if he was off his leash and big like a Doberman."

"Don't be so sure." Nicholas opened his mouth to say more but shut it again.

Pru looked closely at Nicholas. "What do you mean?" she asked. "Are you okay? You're acting dopey."

"I've got a stomach-ache." Nicholas knotted his garbage bag and turned toward the path. "Let's get out of here."

On the way home, they heard a voice call out, "You haven't been littering, have you?" It was Skye Forrest, who lived in a cabin in Deep Woods.

She stared at Clara, who was carrying tinsel and some paper daisies.

"Oh, no," Clara denied. "I was building something."

Skye Forrest gave her a strange look and walked away.

What was that all about? Pru wondered.

CHAPTER SIX

WHISPERS

It was the next day. School was almost over. The *slap, slap* of waves on the shore carried through the window, and a breeze, smelling of sea salt, lifted the edge of Pru's paper. She pencilled AUGUSTA, the capital, onto her Maine map and moved over to help Sophie, who was looking at postcards of Seal Island in the olden days and adding words like "farm" and "sheep" to her vocabulary list. Today they had started their

Maine history projects. Nicholas and Clara were whispering as they unrolled a wide strip of white paper and tacked it to one wall for the class mural.

They've been whispering all afternoon. How come? Pru asked herself. Nicholas had been acting jumpy all day, too. He got in and out of his seat, tapped his pencil, and kept looking at his watch. He had even pushed Gander away when the dog wagged his way up to him, looking for a scratch. Nicholas never ignored Gander.

Miss Sparling stopped at Pru's table. "Thanks for helping Sophie with her writing."

"You're welcome," Pru said, thinking how much she liked her teacher. "For the mural, can I do the English ship that discovered Seal Island?"

"Of course," said Miss Sparling. "That was the—"

"*Archangel* in 1605." Harry liked to show off what he knew about boats. "But before that were the Vikings. I want to make Viking ships."

"It's not fair!" Clara's voice carried across the

room. Pru saw Nicholas shake his head. "Sssh!" she heard him say.

"That's enough paper," Miss Sparling told Clara and Nicholas. "You can put the rest away."

Nicholas turned around. As soon as he saw Pru watching, he busied himself with the paper, stacked the roll on its end in a corner, and sat down at his desk without looking up. What is going on? Pru wondered. They'd never had secrets from each other before.

"Thank you, everyone, for your good work today." Miss Sparling smiled at the class. "We'll start the mural Monday."

Sophie rang the dismissal bell and everyone crowded into the entrance hall to put on their jackets. Pru turned to Nicholas and Clara. "Can you come over?" she asked, dying to know what was going on.

"Nope, sorry," Nicholas mumbled.

"I have to help my dad at the fish house." Clara snatched her backpack and she and Nicholas hurried out the door.

Pru felt awful. "Is she mad about something?" she asked Sophie.

"Maybe about me. I sneaked up to the cupola," Sophie said. "*I'll* come over."

"I forgot. I'm busy," Pru lied, and scuffed her way along the path to the main road.

Pru didn't feel like going home alone. Her mom would ask where Clara and Nicholas were, and Pru didn't want to tell her that they had gone off without her.

She sat down on the library steps not far from the school. How come her friends were acting so strange? She peered into the grass by her feet. Maybe she'd find a four-leaf clover. That would change her luck. But she only saw three-leafers.

Determined to keep looking, she crossed the road into a meadow dotted with blue asters. Everything had grown so high that she couldn't find any clovers at all. She kept going until the path intersected a trail that led into a distant part of the woods.

Here tiny shafts of light filtered through the branches onto the pine needles under her feet.

She climbed over a tree that had fallen across the trail and sat down under a giant hemlock. Feathery hemlock seedlings dotted the forest floor. She breathed in the smell of pine and damp moss. This is a good-luck place, she thought.

Kneeling, Pru began a house of twigs and bark. She carefully built up the sides and then the flat roof. Inside she set a twig bed and two pebble chairs. Then she took two pennies from her pocket and left them in the doorway.

"I wish Clara and Nicholas would tell me their secret," she said. "And I wish we'd all be best friends."

The wishes made her feel better. "And please don't let anything happen to *this* house," she finished.

She stood up, ready to walk on. Suddenly, something moved in the hemlock grove. A dark shape slipped behind a tree. Then Pru heard a snapping sound. It's just a deer stepping on a fallen branch, she thought.

She waited, hoping the deer would walk toward her. But no deer showed its pointed ears.

She brushed pine needles from her hands and knees. A branch snapped again.

They're not usually so shy, Pru thought. She walked along the path, not wanting to go home just yet, and listened to the waves thunder against the rocky cliff at the trail's end. Soon she would have crossed to the other side of the narrow island. A chickadee landed on a bush in front of her, sang, and flew away.

Then she heard what sounded like a sneeze.

Pru spun around. What was *that?* A person? No, it couldn't be. She knew everyone on the island. All fifty-six of them. None of them would hide in the woods.

Maybe the photographer had come back, and she had missed seeing him come ashore. No, Nicholas or Doug or someone would have told her. Besides, why would he hide? It didn't make sense.

Unless . . . unless . . . the sneeze might be . . . Pru's heart thumped faster . . . the fairy house smasher!

I'm not scared, Pru told herself. But Mom will wonder where I am. She began to run.

Just before the trail opened again into the sunny meadow, Pru saw one of her neighbors. Mrs. Bowdoin was on the trails committee and often in the woods, clearing brush, replacing trail markers, and bird watching.

"Did you just hear something strange?" Pru asked.

"Strange how?" Mrs. Bowdoin focused her binoculars on a small gray bird walking head first down a tree trunk.

"Footsteps. Snapping noises. In the trees."

"Probably deer," said Mrs. Bowdoin.

"It sneezed."

"Deer sneeze."

"Maybe," said Pru, unconvinced. "Did you know some fairy houses have been knocked over?"

"Oh?" replied Mrs. Bowdoin. "Well, not everyone likes them. They intrude on the natural world. For another thing, making them tears up the moss, and it takes a long time to grow back."

"I don't use moss," Pru was quick to say.

"Well, not everyone is as careful as you, my dear. Some people even use foil and plastic." Mrs. Bowdoin made a *tsk, tsking* sound like a squirrel. "That's littering."

Uh-oh, Pru thought. She was sure Mrs. Bowdoin would not like Clara's palace. Maybe she's the stomper. She wanted to ask, but she didn't dare.

She had to warn Clara and Nicholas. Someone or something was definitely out there. And it wasn't a Doberman after all.

CHAPTER SEVEN

SNICKERS BARS
AND SECRETS

The next day right after breakfast, Pru bridled
Velvet and trotted bareback down Main Street,
Schooner walking beside her. Nicholas always
helped in the store on Saturdays. Overnight
she had decided to talk to him first without
Clara.

Overhead the sky was as blue as the piece of
sea glass in her treasure box. "Indian summer,"

she told her pony. "I know, 'cause Miss Sparling said so."

Pru waved to Mr. Clarke, who stood on his porch with its missing steps. He spooned cat food into a row of saucers. She often stopped to bring him cookies she had baked. "That's real nice of you, Pru," he always said. Now she watched him clump in and out the front door, his boots shaking the rickety floorboards.

Then she slowed Velvet and studied Mr. Clarke's feet. His boots looked big enough to match Clara's drawing. He couldn't be the stomper, could he?

No, she decided. He was too nice. Besides, Mr. Clarke liked fairy houses. She knew he had built them when he was little.

"Hi, Pru," Mr. Clarke greeted her. "Good to have the island to ourselves now that summer's over." Mr. Clarke hated the day trippers. They dropped candy wrappers, stepped on the wildflowers, and got lost on the trails. "Wish the tourists would visit Mars instead of Maine," he grumbled.

Pru smiled. Mr. Clarke would probably be happiest if he lived all alone on Seal Island with just his cats for company.

At the store Pru tied Velvet to a porch post and opened the screen door. Inside, the big room smelled of coffee beans, raw fish, and spicy barbecue sauce from the rotisserie. On Saturdays nearly everyone on the island bought barbecued chicken for supper. Nicholas sat on the floor unpacking a carton of grapefruit juice.

"May I help you?" asked Mr. Lansing-Ross. Nicholas's father liked to pretend Pru was an important customer.

"Two Snickers bars," Nicholas answered for her. "One for Pru and one for me." Pru thought it was wonderful to have a store and be able to ask for whatever you wanted.

"Yes, sir!" Mr. Lansing-Ross rang up the sale on the register. Even though Nicholas could help himself, his father kept a record and Nicholas had to pay by working.

Pru liked Nicholas's father and was glad he had bought the store when Mr. Farnum retired last year. Nicholas's mother worked there, too, when she wasn't painting pictures of rocks and waves or writing letters to the governor about protecting the environment.

"Thanks for the candy." Pru peeled back the wrapper. "Can I help?" Nicholas nodded and she began to line up cans on the juice shelf just as fast as he unpacked them. Last spring they had worked in the store to earn money to buy Gander

for Miss Sparling. They knew just what to do. It's nice to be here again helping, Pru thought. I won't say anything about secrets and fairy houses yet.

The door banged open and Miss Sparling and Andy Taylor came in, talking and laughing. He was the carpenter who was fixing up Miss Sparling's house. He took off his tool belt and set it on the counter.

"Do you think she likes him?" Pru whispered to Nicholas. "He's really cute. Like someone in the movies." Pru had been to the movies twice in Ellsworth.

"How would I know?" Nicholas said. "I'm not clairvoyant."

"Pu-leeze," Pru said. "I don't read as many books as you do."

"It means I can't see into Miss Sparling's brain."

"I think she likes him," guessed Pru. "Maybe they'll get married."

"I'm never getting married." Nicholas slit open another carton of juice with his Swiss army knife. "It would interfere with my work."

Pru was secretly disappointed. She had thought she might marry Nicholas when she grew up. "What work?"

"I've decided I'm going to be a paleontologist. You have to study for a zillion years."

"What's a paleo . . . whatever?" Pru asked.

"They find fossils of carnivorous reptiles like dinosaurs."

"I still want to see the dinosaurs in the museum that you told me about," Pru reminded him.

Nicholas looked doubtful. "I don't think the school can afford a field trip to New York City."

"I'm not giving up," Pru insisted.

Miss Sparling and Andy Taylor bought a barbecued chicken and left together. "See," Pru said. "She's having him over for lunch."

"My mom says, if you work in the store, you know everything about Seal Island." Nicholas stood up. "More than you should." He stacked his empty cartons inside one another and carried them to the back room.

Pru followed him. "Well, listen to this!" she

said. "I heard a strange noise yesterday in the woods."

Nicholas hesitated. "Oh? What did you hear?"

"Something or someone was behind the trees. I heard a sneeze. Then I saw Mrs. Bowdoin. She told me some people don't like fairy houses. Do you think she could be the stomper?"

Nicholas gulped and glanced away. "I don't know. Maybe."

"You're acting funny." Pru's words spilled out. "What were you and Clara whispering about yesterday? Is it a secret?"

"Uh . . . yes." Nicholas took two steps toward the back door of the store, like he wanted to leave.

"Well, aren't you going to tell me?" Maybe Clara and Nicholas had solved the mystery without her.

Nicholas looked around for his father, who was in the front of the store helping a customer. "Quiet," he whispered. Then he spoke in his regular voice. "When I'm done working, want to look for whales at Blueberry Point? They're migrating."

Pru stared at Nicholas. How could he talk about whales? "Don't change the subject!" She stamped her foot and then slammed the storage room door. Nicholas jumped back and hit a box of soda cans. They clattered to the floor.

"Don't be mad, Pru," he said. "Please! You're my best friend. You don't know what a predicament I'm in. Wait for me outside! I'll tell you everything."

CHAPTER EIGHT

BAD NEWS

Pru rode Velvet back and forth outside the store, first walking, then trotting, trying to make the time pass faster. What did Nicholas mean? What predicament? Why didn't he want his father to hear?

Doug and Max waved to Pru from the harbor's edge. The tide was out and the wet sand flats glimmered in the sun. "We're burying gold coins," Doug yelled.

"They're fake." Max held a coin above his head. "We're going to fool people."

"Well, I wouldn't advertise it!" Pru couldn't help smiling, even though her stomach had that tied-up-in-knots feeling.

Harry was on the beach, too, sanding his dory in front of the wooden shed where the fishermen stored their day's catches.

"Have you heard about the fairy houses?" Pru asked, reining in the pony. Harry's dog, Snuffles, growled at Schooner and went on chewing a fishhead coated with sand.

"Yup." Harry wasn't worried. He thought fairy houses were silly. He had stopped building them in first grade.

"Do you know who's knocking them over?"

"It's Snuffles."

"No joking, Harry," said Pru. "This is serious."

"Actually, I think it's Miss Sparling. Or—" Harry eyeballed Velvet—"it might be Funny Four-Legs here."

"Cut it out!" Pru stroked her pony's neck. "Never!"

"Here comes Mr. Dictionary." Harry glanced up as Nicholas ran toward them.

"Come on." Nicholas took hold of Velvet's bridle. "We have to get Clara."

"Not me." Harry rubbed his sandpaper along the dory's sides. "I'm sticking with boats."

"Ride behind," Pru directed. Nicholas climbed on the pony's back. "Why do we need Clara?"

"You'll see," was all Nicholas would say. "But you can't take Velvet."

Just before the road forked near Pru's house, Nicholas slid off. "Meet me on Spruce Trail," he told her and ran up the hill.

Pru jogged Velvet into his stall and hung up his bridle. "Mom!" she called as she pushed her dog in the front door. "Will you watch Schooner? I'm going to Deep Woods."

She caught up with Nicholas at the LEASH YOUR DOG sign. "This is crazy!" She gulped for breath. "You've *got* to tell me what's happening."

But Nicholas raced along the path until he reached the woodland fairy houses.

"I'm not going another step until you—" Pru stopped short.

There was Clara. She knelt on the ground in front of her palace, with ribbons, tinsel, and sticks scattered around her.

"No!" Pru cried. "Not again!"

Clara turned toward them, her face smudged with tears.

"It's not what you think," said Nicholas.

With one sweep of her hand Clara demolished the top story and the rest of the building tumbled in on itself.

"What are you doing?" For one awful moment Pru thought that Clara was the mysterious stomper.

Nicholas tried to explain. "I told her to do it, because I found out who the stompers are. And I didn't want them to get it."

"What? You know? It's not just one?" Pru desperately wanted to know, too. "Who *are* they?"

Nicholas answered so softly Pru could hardly hear him. "My mother, for one."

"Your mother? That's totally crazy," Pru said. "You're making it up." Why on earth would his mother do a thing like that?

"Well, she and Mrs. Bowdoin and Skye Forrest and Mr. Clarke."

"Mr. Clarke?" Pru could not believe what she was hearing.

"They don't like the mess fairy houses are making in the woods," Nicholas said. "They say people are littering."

"But we've always made them!" Pru was in shock.

"Yeah, but now people are making huge ones. They tear branches off trees and yank up moss."

"Did you know about this?" Pru asked Clara, who was salvaging bits and pieces of her palace and shoving them in her backpack.

"Not until Nicholas told me at school." Clara wiped her eyes with the back of her hand. "It's not fair. If other people build them, I don't see why I can't."

"Mom had already told me the day Clara built the palace," Nicholas said. "But I was scared to tell you."

"No wonder you didn't like it." Clara frowned at him. "If you'd said something then about the stompers, you could have saved me a lot of work."

"I know my mom wants to save whales and trees and everything, but I didn't expect her to do anything this crazy." Nicholas rushed on, as if he wanted to get it over with. "I knew they wouldn't like your house, Clara. I didn't want them to knock it over if they went out again. So I told you first."

Pru was starting to understand. "Did you tell her yesterday at school?" she asked. "Is that what you were whispering about?"

Nicholas and Clara nodded.

I feel better, Pru thought. At least they weren't angry at me. But . . . how come Nicholas didn't tell me, too?

"I wanted to tell you," Nicholas said before Pru could ask. "But I knew you'd be mad."

"I am mad. I'm mad at the people who don't

like fairy houses. But I'm not mad at you."

"I'm mad, too!" Clara heaved a stone into the bushes.

"I bet it was Mrs. Bowdoin hiding in the woods that day." Pru felt dumb for not figuring it out sooner. "I should have known."

"My mother's having a meeting Sunday at the school." Nicholas groaned. "Now the whole town will know what she did."

Pru was startled. "A meeting? About the fairy houses?"

"Yup," said Nicholas. "She's inviting everyone."

"That's awful! I feel sorry for you," Clara told him. "With a mother like that."

Nicholas's temper flared. "Hey! My mother's okay. She cares about nature, that's all."

"So do I," Clara said in a hurry. "I just didn't think what I was doing was wrong." She tried to pat the moss she had used back into the ground.

"That's always the problem," Nicholas said.

"What are we going to do now?" Pru asked.

CHAPTER NINE

INVISIBLE
AS THE FAIRIES

"What if they say no fairy houses ever again?" Pru
wondered as she and her parents walked to the
schoolhouse for the meeting.

"We could move," her mother teased. She carried a carrot cake heaped with orange frosting.

"No way! I'm never leaving!"

"I'm with you," her dad said, giving her a
quick squeeze.

Inside the school Nicholas's mother, Mr. Clarke, and Mrs. Bowdoin were next to each other in the front row. Skye Forrest stood in the back. The guilty ones, thought Pru. Max, Doug, and Doug's parents sat close to Miss Sparling.

"Harry's here," Pru said to her dad. "I didn't think he'd come." Nicholas sat on the floor, scrunched in a corner, behind Harry. Pru felt bad for him. It must be embarrassing to have your mother do something like that and then call a meeting to tell everyone.

"Look! There's that photographer!" Pru pointed him out to her parents as he set his camera bags down beside the goldfish tank. "How come he's here?"

But before anyone could explain, Nicholas's mother stood up and the room grew silent. She held a box in her hands, which overflowed with what Pru guessed were old fairy house decorations. Plastic ribbons and tinsel hung down one side. Soda cans and bottles poked over the top.

"This is a sample of what we have been finding in the woods." Mrs. Lansing-Ross spoke in a loud, clear voice. "Last week in an attempt to dramatize the problem, some of us went out and knocked down the fairy houses that were the most egregious examples of disregard for the environment. And we collected this to show you."

"She talks like Nicholas," Pru whispered to Clara, who had come in with Sophie and taken the seat beside her.

"With the large number of visitors who hike in our beautiful woods and then build fairy houses, we have a problem. It's not just children. It's adults, too. The houses are getting bigger and more elaborate."

"Whoops," Clara said quietly and looked down at the floor.

"Hear! Hear!" Mr. Clarke raised his hands over his head and clapped. Mrs. Bowdoin clapped, too.

"I, for one, think the fairy houses should go," Mrs. Lansing-Ross continued. "We are harming the ecology of the island, damaging trees, digging holes, killing moss. And we are allowing people to litter our forest floor with plastic, metal, and other things that take hundreds of years to biodegrade, if they ever do."

More clapping. Uh-oh, thought Pru. We're losing.

Next Mrs. Bowdoin said a few words. "As you know, I am on the trails committee." Her bluebird earrings flew back and forth as she moved her head. "The wear and tear on the trails increases every year. We need some rules here. And the first rule I suggest is that we ban fairy house building altogether."

This time a few voices cheered. Others booed.

Pru's father waited for the audience to quiet down. "I understand your concerns," he said, "but fairy houses have been a tradition here since I was a kid. I'd hate to lose that tradition."

Hooray for my dad! thought Pru.

"I second that," said Harry's father.

"I double-second it," called out Miss Sparling.

"I built 'em, too, when I was a youngster." Today Mr. Clarke wore a white shirt under his red suspenders. "But in those days only a couple of us kids did. Now there's so many trippers, you can't step onto your porch without somebody asking where a toilet is or the way to the woods."

Pru and Clara giggled.

"I think we should only allow one sightseeing boat a day to come to the island." Skye Forrest spoke now. "Two boats bring too many people."

"Wait a minute!" roared Mr. Nickerson, who owned the *Happy Whale,* one of the boats. "Are you telling me I can't earn a living here?"

"I'm against any rules." Doug's dad didn't shout, but he didn't talk softly either. Pru could tell he was upset. "We don't want to discourage tourists. They buy our lobsters. And your paintings," he reminded Nicholas's mother and Skye Forrest, who were both artists.

Mrs. Lansing-Ross looked annoyed and then tried to smile. "Other comments, please?"

Pru glanced at her parents. They nodded. Okay, here goes. In June she had talked at the end-of-school celebration. She could do it again.

"Kids like fairy houses." Her voice sounded wobbly. "I think we should keep them." She felt Clara poke her and heard her whisper, "Good!" Pru went on. "We could all promise to make little ones with only things we find in the woods. But no moss and no plastic stuff."

"My guests like to build big, fancy houses," said Mrs. Horne, who rented rooms to vacationers. "Instead of telling them no, why don't we organize clean-ups every so often?"

There were groans from the audience. "Lady, get a life," a man bellowed. "We've got fishing to do."

To Pru's surprise, Nicholas spoke from his corner. "We need a publicity campaign."

"How would that work?" asked Mr. Clarke.

"We can let people know about the problem and ask them to help. I'll make a poster that says DON'T LITTER for the store."

"People don't read," Mr. Clarke complained.

"People look at pictures." Harry walked to the

front of the room. Wow, thought Pru, how come he's so brave? "I've got another idea," he said. "My dad and I will make a sign with a humongous fairy house on it. And then cross it out with a big line. You know, like 'a big house is a no-no.'"

"I like it!" Skye Forrest exclaimed from the back.

Pru felt a rush of affection for Harry. For someone who thought fairy houses were for babies, that was a nice thing to do. The thought of signs gave her an idea. She waved her hand.

"There's more." Harry seemed to enjoy having everyone watch him. "Next to the big house will be a little house. One hundred percent natural. With no line through it."

"Does that mean twig houses are okay?" Doug asked from his seat.

"Yes," said Nicholas's mother. "Thank you, Harry. Signs would help."

Pru jumped up. "May I speak, please?" She wasn't scared now. Well, only a little. Mrs. Lansing-Ross nodded.

"Here's my idea." Pru's mind was racing. "A

sign for my pony. Two signs, really, to go over his back and hang down each side. And," she stopped for breath, hoping people would like the next and best part, "I'll write on them: PROTECT OUR WOODS. MAKE YOUR FAIRY HOUSES AS INVISIBLE AS THE FAIRIES."

"That's a wonderful suggestion," Pru heard Miss Sparling say.

"And what will you do with your pony?" asked Mrs. Lansing-Ross.

"Take Velvet to meet the boat and around the island. So everyone will see him."

This time the whole room clapped. Pru sat down, her heart thudding.

"Great idea!" Clara was impressed. "I'll help you."

"Me, too," said Sophie.

"Thanks," Pru said, thinking that even if Clara was a little bossy now and then, she really liked her.

Mr. Nickerson's voice boomed again. "The kids have solved the problem to my satisfaction. Now can I get back to work?"

"Are we in favor of trying the kids' solution?" Mrs. Lansing-Ross asked.

"Aye," everyone shouted.

"The trails committee will have to make sure people obey the signs." Mrs. Bowdoin sounded worried.

"We can do it," said Skye Forrest.

"If everything is settled, it's time for refreshments." Pru's mother pointed to her cake, which waited on a corner table.

"Thank you for your help," said Mrs. Lansing-Ross. "The meeting is adjourned."

The children gathered around the cake. "I'm proud of you," Miss Sparling said as she cut slices.

"I don't believe it." Doug faked a punch to his head. "Dumb me! It wasn't that dog after all."

"Our detective work bombed," Max said.

The photographer walked up to them. He smiled at Pru. "I wanted to tell you that my dog didn't knock down any fairy houses. I heard you at the ferry, but I don't think you heard me."

"Thank you," Pru said, surprised that he was so nice.

"I'm putting something about the fairy houses in my magazine story. Is it okay if I photograph you?"

"Can we all be in it?"

"Of course," he said.

"One second!" Pru ran to her desk "Get your lighthouses for the picture!"

"Did they bring us good luck or not?" Clara asked.

"Maybe yes, maybe no," said Nicholas. "All we know is we saved the genuine, old-time dwellings for the fairy folk." He lifted his lighthouse in a salute. "Hooray for the Seal Island seven!"

Harry whistled and all of them stamped their feet. The camera flashed.

"More cake, please," said Sophie.

Everyone took second helpings, including Pru, who was already thinking ahead. She would make sure her signs for Velvet were just right.

"I hope you come back next summer," Pru said to the photographer. "My pony will be six then and he'd like to have his picture taken."

"Wearing his PROTECT OUR WOODS signs?"

"Right!" Pru grinned. "We'll meet you at the boat."